MODERN GREEK WRITERS

GIOCONDA

The translation costs of this book have been covered
by the Organisation for the Cultural Capital of Europe
"Thessaloniki 1997".

Typeset in Greece
by Photokyttaro Ltd.
14, Armodiou St., Athens 105 52
Tel. 32.44.111
and printed by
M. Monteverdis & P. Alexopoulos
Metamorphosis, Athens
For
Kedros Publishers, S.A.,
3, G. Gennadiou St., Athens 106 78,
Tel. 38.09.712 – Fax 38.31.981
July 1997

Title in Greek: Τζιοκόντα
Cover design by Dimitris Kalokyris

© *1975 by N.A. Kokantzis*
© *1997 by Kedros Publishers, S.A.*
Athens, Greece

ISBN 960-04-1344-4

NIKOS A. KOKANTZIS

Gioconda

Translated into English
by the author

KEDROS

The story that follows is true.

LAST NIGHT I DREAMT OF MY OLD NEIGHBOURHOOD again. A dream in my sleep, a nightmare when I am awake and see what has become of it. But I've known it in its glory, I've known it as it was of old. How lucky I was to have been born and raised there in those days before the War, to have lived there through the War and the Occupation. And for some years afterwards.

In those days, before the War, in areas like ours, people still lived in houses and not in blocks of flats; there were gardens and flowers and the seasons of the year had their own individual scent each, the quiet of the night was broken only by the barking of a dog and the crowing of a rooster before dawn, the frogs croaked in the pool at the neighbour's courtyard in the summer, the milkman called early in the morning, there was the first cheerful gossip of the women at their gardens' fences. There were no cars. God, all this – and so much more besides.

There was, at that time, a poor little house that was to become very important to me. Long and low-built, it had a sloping roof and a vine that covered half the front and sprawled all over the porch. On one side it looked onto a so-called garden with two or three flower-pots, grass and weeds but also a big fig-tree, a decrepit fence that just marked the boundaries rather than protected the garden – not that there was anything to protect or anyone to protect it from – a garden, in other words, that was honest and unpretentious, made a little bit by man and mostly by God, a joy to behold. In the years that followed and are now gone, as I wandered in the parks of Europe, my heart bled for it, and I felt a longing for its obscure corners, the boulders the beetles the grasshoppers the lizards, the limitless world that was enclosed in its few hand-spreads of land, where we played and grew up and lived and came to know – above all where we came to know.

So.

In between that little house and our own, there was an open plot of land, overgrown with wild grass in the summer; we never knew to whom it belonged as nobody had ever claimed it and this was where our little gang used to gather together, a place to talk, to play, to quarrel, to love. There we played hide-and-seek, cops and robbers, there we pretended to be explorers in the jungle, there, in the summer evenings, we lay on the grass and spoke of things that mattered.

Those of us who met there almost every day were my two first cousins and myself and the six children of the family that owned the little house. The first four of them were girls, the two younger ones boys. There were, naturally, differences of age between us all but, for a long period of time, this didn't matter and we all played together.

They were Jews and very poor, a fact which was cheerfully ignored by their parents. Anyhow, in those days and in our world there were no striking differences in the way families lived. There was an old grandmother, too, who must have seen better days in her life and who behaved with a nobility of manner that went well with her looks. She spoke in a low commanding voice and made you feel that she expected the courteous bow, the kissing of her hand. And yet she was not cold nor did one feel uncomfortable in her presence. On the contrary, one was attracted by her and ready to fall in with her. She was genuine.

Her daughter and her son-in-law, the parents of our friends, were much more simple people. But they had a natural gentleness of manner which, together with their warm hospitality, made one love them – even though one was often, quite good-naturedly, inclined to laugh at them a little. What made the whole thing quite amusing was that, in spite of their poverty, they had a perfect right to show off in some ways. They possessed things which were not to be found in much richer homes in Salonika at that time. To begin with, their house, such as it was, was their own and not rented as was the case with most people then. Only the very rich had their own private homes. Then they had a piano in their house, a very rare possession for a poor family. It had been with them for no one knew how many years and had certainly not been tuned for as long. But it was there. And the children were always going to start taking lessons, in fact the two elder daughters played tolerably well. And when Madame Leonora, their mother, would frequently come out to the porch and call them, perhaps just a little bit too loudly, to come in and have tea and then study their piano lesson, no one could say she was being anything but a good mother. Which was, indeed, exactly what she was.

The children had taken after her, they had her big brown beautiful eyes with the warm smiling expression. Only Gioconda, the fourth in line and one year younger than I, had hazel eyes, slightly slanting, with an expression that was often grave, almost sad. She was a beautiful girl. Tall and well-made, with slow sensual movements, the world lit up when she smiled. She was my companion when we played and how proud I was when I happened to hear that she spoke frequently about me to her mother – my ears would pick up such comments passing between Madame Leonora and my Mother – she was always on my side. She would pick a quarrel on my behalf while I, out of timidity and a natural gentleness of manner, or mere indifference, would not insist on something or other. On such moments, rather infrequent to tell the truth, her usual shyness would give way to a fiery behaviour that surprised us all and she would have her way – which was mine to begin with. Neither she nor I knew then what this must have meant already. She was my closest companion, from the time we learned how to talk to the time when, at fifteen, she was taken away, with all her family, by the Germans. Two years before that, she was the first girl in my life to smile up at me, suddenly and without any foretelling, with a smile that was totally different from any I had known until then, the meaning of which she couldn't have known herself, raising her eyes to mine for a brief moment, in the half-darkness of an evening in springtime, as we stood, somewhat awkwardly, under the apricot-tree in our garden, a fleeting shy smile while my mind became dizzy from an unknown excitement.

We both used to invent games of our own or change the rules of the established ones. An unspoken competition had started between us and we felt pleasure in outdoing one another in originality. We needed to be constantly together. We played, the two of us, from the time I hadn't yet started to pay any particular attention to her, we played when I was seven and eight and she six and seven, we played when I was twelve and she eleven and already important to me and I her hero. I had only to speak to her and she would turn crimson. Her family had noticed this and were amused; only we two knew nothing yet, were just happy to be together, with an intensity that increased with the passage of time, into almost a fury; it must have been the most intense substitute for love play at a time when we didn't even know what we were made of.

CAME THE WAR AND THEN THE OCCUPATION AND I WAS thirteen and then fourteen and she had begun to develop almost from when she was eleven, a sensual expression on her face and her movements and gestures had a feminine grace that was not lost when she entered puberty, so at twelve she was already a woman in every small beautiful part of her body, her eyes her voice her manners – and, at the same time, incredibly and excitingly innocent and sweet.

All the family were handsome people. The grandmother with her severe long face, the pale skin and the rich white hair; Madame Leonora, and her eldest daughter Laura, who was almost her carbon-copy, with their old-time beauty, the big romantic eyes, the small mouth, the shy smile; Jack, the father, tall, grizzled, strong, with a kindly face and the heart of a child;

Renée, the second daughter, juicy, full of life, with teasing eyes, very feminine, terrribly attractive and well aware of the fact; Aline, thin and pale, a transparent face, with very delicate health and frequently unwell, most of the time sitting in an armchair which they placed in the garden during the summer and by the wood-burning stove in the winter, a book in her hand and a faraway look in her eyes which seemed to be gazing at a future that she would never see. And then Gioconda, my Gioconda, the best of them all. Last came the two boys, Peppo, with the longest eye-lashes I have ever seen fluttering over his brown warm eyes and Maurice, a mischievous little devil, tiny but strong.

This was Gioconda's family and they were lovable.

Yet there was for me, at that time, a black mark, a source of worry and discomfort. And this was a cousin of Gioconda's, two years older than I, Rudi was his name, tall and attractive, and aware of the fact, and I disliked him and he knew this too and seemed amused. He visited the family much too often for my liking and he was particularly attentive to Gioconda, or at least that's how it came to seem to me after a certain point in time, and jealousy never left my heart after that. Worse still, I had to admit that he was better than I in many ways and he liked to show off his various talents. He was slim but strong with swift and easy movements. Intelligent and a good talker, he knew funny stories and told them well and made everybody laugh. As if all this was not enough – half of it would have been plenty – he also played the guitar and sang with a soft voice when mine was still like a croak and often broke in the middle of a sentence, changing into too high or too low a pitch and making me feel a fool. In other words, he was near perfect and I had to admit it and he knew it and he made sure that everybody else knew it, too. In other words I hated him. Little by little he became like an obsession, a sort of nightmare, and I was convinced I could not possibly compete with him. I became suspicious of every little sign, I found a deeper meaning in every little word, everything took on a particular significance in my troubled mind and became proof that she preferred him to me, that she admired him. Therefore she must be in love with him. The moment I reached that terrible conclusion I was lost in a deep despair. Which made me do a shameful thing one day, I feel ashamed of it to this day, yet which, as it later proved, was to speed up matters in my favour. He was visiting them, one hot summer day, he had actually had lunch with them; I had seen him come and knew he was going to stay, so I could not eat, my throat was a tight knot and my stomach felt turned inside out. I sat at the table and thought, miserably, how at that very moment, he was sitting at *their* table and how he must be telling his funny stories again and making them hang from his lips and how she must be looking at him with admiration, never thinking of me even for a moment, or, if she did, only to compare me with him and find me totally lacking in charm. Yes, that's how it must be, I had no doubt at all. Plain as sunlight it was. And the more I thought of it all, the more I saw his triumph, the deeper sank my heart. My mouth was dry and bitter. Not a single mouthful could I eat, pretending I had a stomach upset, not even pretending but telling the truth, till the moment came when I could stand it no longer and I got up from the table and went to my room and lay on my bed. I lay there, my body inert but my brain spinning, as the heat of the summer afternoon entered through the closed shutters and the open windows, together with the sound of the cicadas in the garden and a salty smell from the sea, faint but inviting, I, lying there, not moving, all naked and soaked in perspiration, wanting to cry but not allowing myself to do so, lay there all the long summer afternoon, when everybody else slept, no sound coming from anybody anywhere, those same hours when, on another day, that same summer heat, the half-light of the shuttered room and my naked body would have filled my imagination – had done so for more than a year now – with fantasies of love that I had never experienced; naked women, their bodies there for me to touch to caress everywhere their hands to touch me in turn, my hardened body, kisses all over, erotic scenes, nebulous and unbearably exciting.

Only this day my body was flaccid, my mind lost. Jealousy and hatred were gnawing at my insides. And all the time I felt totally helpless and defeated. The lazy afternoon slowly cooled off and finally gave way to the fragrant evening. The shadows asserted their rights on earth. This was the hour we usually came out from our homes, like insects in the dark, and gathered together in the open plot to spend ourselves in play. When I found the courage to go out and meet them, Gioconda, Rudi and Peppo were standing outside their front door, talking to a couple of friends from the neighbourhood. I joined them trying to look unconcerned and friendly. Rudi was most courteous to me from the start, too courteous it seemed to me, so my confused and suspicious mind decided that he was treating me with that sort of condescension that a victor has for those he has defeated or knows he can defeat if only he chooses to do so. This impression didn't help my mood at all, of course. When it also seemed to me that Gioconda was much too silent and avoiding my eyes – therefore undoubtedly guilty – I went to pieces. Everything was now quite plain. Gioconda was in love with Rudi and that made her feel guilty towards me. Rudi knew it and that made him feel triumphant towards me. All this was too much. I could not endure it. No matter what they did or said, no matter what I did or said, trying to appear cool and natural, there was a heavy pressure at the back of my head and my stomach felt as if it was gripped by a cruel hand. Every now and then I had to take deep breaths. As for Gioconda and Rudi, their slightest gesture, anything they said, an imperceptible change in the tone of their voice or in the expression of their face, a passing look, everything, seemed to me to have its own particular significance, its hidden meaning. There could be no doubt, they were in love. I tried to be reasonable. I told myself I was being silly, I was imagining things, there was nothing to it, for everything that seemed suspect to me there must surely be an explanation – all this I told myself again and again. No good. No sooner would I feel some relief than my attention would be drawn to some new proof that my fears were right and all my own arguments would break down like a dam giving way to the pressure of rising water. My brain was drowned under the waves of my jealousy, my knees were like jelly. I felt an immense pity for myself, I felt lonely and deserted. And humiliated. This was the first taste of failure and it was very bitter.

I took part, quite mechanically, in the game the others had started, unconscious of what I was doing, my mind all taken up by my loss. It was odd how, in those few hours, I realized, very clearly, the extent of my feelings for her. All the things I wanted to do and share with her, images that fused together, shapes and colours, a life with her, all was now soaked in a warm, almost liquid sadness that was also very sweet. I wanted to sit down on a little rock, alone, the scent of thyme filling the evening air, and weep until my heart was softened. And as I thought of it, I let myself imagine that, as I would be sitting there, alone, I would suddenly feel a hand touching my face and I would turn my head and there she would be, silent and loving, in the dusk, waiting. A shot of joy would go through me at this fantasy but the next moment I would feel worse than before, the ugliness of reality would hit me again and I would know that nothing like this would ever happen, of course, that if I sat down on a little rock, alone, the scent of thyme filling the evening air, to weep, the whole thing would end, very simply, with me sitting down on a little rock, alone, the scent of thyme filling the air, weeping. This realization only increased my self-pity. And all this time I was fully aware that everything I did or thought or felt, the role I was playing and, possibly, unconsciously enjoying too, was nothing different from the deeds, the words and the emotions, of numberless young boys of my own age, ages before I was born or at the same time with me or in the years and the centuries to come, there and elsewhere and all over the world, that all this had been written already in thousands of stories and poems and songs, good bad or mediocre, had been read or listened to by every man on earth, had been imitated or laughed at, or simply ignored, by the generations and that I, myself, at that very moment, was nothing more than an insignificant, colourless cliché of an adolescent who was suffering the pangs of unrequited love. No originality whatsoever. There were moments when I recovered my old capacity of laughing at myself but these were very brief and then I sank again in the quicksand of my despair. The evening was passing with various, unsuccessful, attempts to play a proper game, the younger ones of the group were in a rebellious mood, Gioconda gave the impression that she was not even there, Rudi was more than ever pleased with himself and full of repulsive charm. More than ever that evening – or so it seemed to me – he went out of his way to be good to me. At first I let him tread on me with his kindness, without reacting. But when this had gone on for much too long and I had wallowed in my misery enough to satisfy even my most masochistic needs, I realized that I just couldn't stand him any longer. Enough was enough. I had reached the limit. He was being a perfect angel of love to me. He was manifestly concerned about me. Anything he said, he said it to me, whenever he wanted to suggest something he first wanted to know if I were agreeable. If I happened to object or if he only thought that I did, he hastened to take it back, whatever it was, admit that it had not been a good idea of his, even apologize to me – yes, to me, the scoundrel, he cared only about me, he didn't think of her, only of me, the hypocrite, as if I didn't see through him. Oh he did it on purpose, I had known this for quite some time now. Just what did he mean with his "Nikos this" and "Nikos that" and his "thanks" and his "I'm so sorry", damn his cheek? Oh I wouldn't let the bastard do this to me any longer, no I wouldn't. Wasn't it enough, for Christ's sake, wasn't it enough that he had won her from me? Did he have to humiliate me, on top of it, with his fake unbearable hypocritical manners? This was too much, oh much too much. I would show him what I thought of him. I would cut him short, yessir, I would put him in his place, I would. Thinking how I would get even with him, gave me a sort of relief. Imperceptibly I stopped thinking of what I wanted to do with Gioconda and began to think of what I wanted to do to him. Not only with words either but with my hands too. I forgot how much stronger than I he was, how much more quick and experienced, I forgot the shape my mind was in and I began to indulge in fantasies where I fought with him and knocked him out cold, just so, with one good one on his impertinent nose, oh I gave it to him, I punched his face in, flat against the back of his damned skull, he would lose his speech, he wouldn't know whether he was coming or going, I would make a fool and a silly idiot of him. And all along the others would be watching me with admiration, she with more than admiration, and in the end she would beg me, out of the kindness of her heart, and with a look full of meaning in her eyes, to take pity on him and to spare him. An anger welled up inside me and blinded me, myriad flames burned, thoughts pushed and pulled at each other in my feverish brain; I was telling him off, I was swearing at him with all the inventiveness of my wounded vanity... I can't tell at what point precisely I came to my senses and realized to my horror that, for God knows how long, I had been talking aloud, without knowing it, thinking my filthy thoughts aloud, all the puss and the venom of my beaten pride pouring forth. Suddenly I became aware of what I was doing; the others had stopped playing and were looking at me in motionless amazement. Rudi was deadly pale and as if turned to stone. Gioconda's eyes, those incredible eyes, were looking, at me with a deep sadness. Everything was frozen except the sadness in her eyes – at that frightful moment when I heard myself say: "... so, you filthy Jew" and my breath was cut short and my head felt full of wool, a momentary faint, then the abrupt turnabout and the running straight home, to my room, to my bed. I fell on it, lifeless, my body paralyzed, only my heart beating madly – until I broke down at last and all the remorse and the agony and the shame rushed out from inside me in endless uncontrollable punishing sobs. Now I knew that I had lost not only the battle and Gioconda but my dignity too and my self-respect, even the right to see her again, let alone be with her, love her. That "... filthy Jew" kept ringing in my ears, shouting my injustice and my cowardice, the way I had hurt not only Rudi – and why hurt even him, God, when I loved him as my friend, I felt this now too quite clearly, I wanted him for my friend more than anybody else – but her too and her family and all the Jews everywhere, the Jews that I liked so much and admired, that I had lived with them some of the happiest moments of my life.

I FELL ASLEEP AS I WAS CRYING AND I DID NOT WAKE UP
again until the next morning, left alone by
Mother who was too discreet to show that she
had any notion that something had happened –
although she must have been wondering. Father
had much more important problems to face.

WHEN I WOKE UP NEXT MORNING I FELT BAD EVEN
before I knew why, a feeling of discomfort in my
stomach and, in the clear harsh light of the day,
what I had done seemed even more hideous and
degrading. I felt like a fugitive hunted for a
crime, only I knew that there was nowhere to
hide to get away from those eyes and what I had
seen in them.

There were moments when I told myself that
I should at least be man enough to go and find
her and apologise to her, not so much to say the
words as to give her the chance to tell me to my
face what she thought of me, to punish me so I
could feel clean. And then go and face Rudi and
the others, too. I must give myself up, without
any defence, to their anger or ridicule, whichever
they chose, so as to lessen the pressure in my
heart. I told myself all this, but I proved too
weak to do it.

Instead, I sneaked out of the house, at a moment when there seemed to be nobody around, neither she nor Rudi nor anyone else who could see me and come and spit in my face. I hurried furtively away, relieved and yet oddly disappointed as if, in reality, I did want somebody to be there and see me and come to spit in my face, his spit like holy water that would wash me clean and redeem me.

I walked away, not stopping until I reached the seafront and there climbed on a familiar little stonewall, where I had spent hours before, alone or with friends, carefree or roused by serious arguments when, even at that age, we had to try and understand life and solve our important philosophical problems, forced to grow up before our time because of the War and the Occupation. So I sat there on the low stonewall and let my eyes wander over the early-morning sea, watching the slow, graceful flying of the sea-gulls, listening with a sad ear to the murmur of the water at my feet. Some fishing-boats were swinging sensually at their anchors, there was the smell of the dry seaweed and the salty air, everything was simple and peaceful, and volcanic.

I HEARD FOOTSTEPS AND I THOUGHT, IRRITABLY, THAT nobody had the right to be there at that time but me, nobody at all, it was my own corner, for God's sake, on that particular day I had the right to have my own little place on earth, all to myself, where I could be left alone with my sin for a little while. And then I thought that, maybe, I didn't have that right even, I had no right whatsoever for anything anywhere and so I got up and turned to go – and Gioconda was there, motionless now, just a few steps away, and I thought my God such things don't happen, it can't be true, and then she smiled her sweet shy smile, so it was true, even if it was more than a miracle, she was standing there, she did not vanish, she was smiling and looking at me, I took a cautious step toward her and again she did not disappear. I stopped and then she came up to me and, blushing to the roots of her hair, took me by the hand, softly, and led me back to the stone-wall where I had been sitting and made me climb on it again and she followed me with an easy graceful movement and she sat next to me, her long legs resting on the wall, knees bent, her arms crossed over them, her body pressing on mine all down her side, looking ahead of her at the fishing-boats, having started to talk even before she had sat down, with a quiet voice, without turning her head and without blushing now, her voice low and husky and caressing, a voice that always said more than the words themselves and made me feel as if lizards were running up and down my spine. "I am sorry for what happened yesterday and for how badly you must be feeling now but if you think that I am angry you are wrong, you know." She went on talking. And she told me then, there, by the sea that was full of a jolly laughter, that she had never cared for Rudi; it was for me that she cared, only she didn't know how I felt for her; that there were moments when she thought that I loved her and then the light was bright but there were other times when she felt sure that I didn't care and then it was cold and dark. She told me how she thought about me during the day and how she thought about me during the night and she could not understand what was happening to her, it was something strange, she only knew that at times she was full of joy and at other times she was drowning in sorrow. She told me all this in her own way, her voice soft and tender. And the sea-gulls danced in the air as I listened to her and the fishing-boats were rocking amorously, there was a song in my head and a peculiar sensation like I was melting away, *who would have thought of this my darling Gioconda*, my heart felt like breaking, I was dizzy and faint. And she went on talking. "If you'd care to know, I was very flattered by what happened yesterday. See how selfish I am?" She gave a short laugh and went on. "I've never liked Rudi, honestly. He is too big for his shoes and a show-off. He wouldn't be in and out of our house if I had any say. But he *is* my cousin, the others seem to like him, so what can I do? You know, I think Grandma doesn't like him any too much either, only she won't show it." She talked and talked, she didn't stop, she had let go and was giving vent to all that was inside her. And I listened and her words were like song and light and coloured crystals. She laughed again. "Poor Rudi, it was the first time in my life that I saw him lost for words. When you left, he turned and looked at me and seemed to expect my sympathy but I said nothing so he left too. To tell the truth I feel sorry for him, in a way." Suddenly she was serious, her voice now grave, her head bent. She was silent for a while. Then very slowly, almost haltingly, she said, "You know, though, I don't think you should have said those words at the end... it wasn't nice. But surely you didn't believe them, did you? At least, not really, the way people often say such things to us, when they are being ugly..." Her voice faded away. The way people say... when they are being ugly... My God, what have we been doing to them, what have they had to put up with from us for thousands of years now, how have they borne it with what we, cowards that we are, have scorned as cowardice on their part, only it is dignity and wisdom, such as we can never understand, or possess. And now I had gone and done exactly the same as all these others, I had been ugly too. "I never..." I stammered, "never... I swear it... I," but she had started talking again, her voice a whisper. "Maybe I should have been angry, only my mind was elsewhere, I could only think of what I had realized about us two, your feelings for me. That's all I cared about. Because you wouldn't have acted the way you did if it were not for me, would you? Oh you can't know for how long I wanted to know this, only I couldn't tell for sure. When we know that all is as we want it, as we need it to be, that we need never have doubted, that what we've been waiting for is here, then everything is warm and bright, there is no care in the world. Like when you haven't had anything to eat for a long time and you think there is nothing left and then you find yourself holding a cake. Do you understand what I mean?" She looked at me and her eyes were waiting. But I was dumb. She kept looking at me and now there was doubt in her eyes. I panicked. "Yes, yes, I understand, sure, yes, of course," I cried finally and felt an utter idiot as I could find nothing better to say, I must have seemed a blind deaf-and-dumb. Yet I was choking inside with all the things I wanted to say. I was lost in a delirium of happiness, a storm of joy. Before she could have time to think me stupid, I asked her, "How did you find me here? How did you know?" and immediately felt an idiot again. "Oh but I am a witch, didn't you know?" Her voice playful now. *Didn't I know... beautiful beloved witch, didn't I know...* And then I felt again how much I loved her, and for how long, and how I wouldn't have known it still perhaps, if it were not for Rudi, wonderful Rudi, God bless you my good friend Rudi. She carried on. "Of course I am a witch. And I can see far away, everything that happens, and, in the night, I ride on my broomstick and I fly anywhere in no time, what can you say to that? And I know too how to prepare magic potions and give them to whom I wish," she was talking now as if she were seeing a dream, "I can even make somebody fall in love with me, if I want to..." she stopped abruptly and went red like a beetroot. "Aha," I teased her, "was it not you who prepared tea the other day when I was visiting your house? Did you do your magic then, too?" She looked at me gratefully for a moment, then turned towards the sea. "I wish I had done it much sooner," she murmured. "Because, you see, I must have drunk the whole magic cup of tea in your house years ago, as far back as I can remember. Who was the witch then?" A flood of tenderness rushed from inside me, my eyes were glazed, my reason was chased away. I had never kissed a girl until then, a fact for which my best friend, a daring young boy, kept nagging at me. And now was the moment, not so as I could face my friend as an equal, not because I had thought about it and was prepared but because, very simply, I suddenly knew that I wanted to kiss her and that I was going to do it then and there.

I turned towards her and put my arm round her neck and pulled her to me and pressed my mouth on hers, all in an abrupt awkward motion, when she was totally unprepared. And so, instead of a soft first kiss which both of us would remember with a thrill for the rest of our lives, my teeth struck on hers, cutting her upper lip, she moaned, pulled herself away and put her hand on her mouth and then looked at it and it was red with blood. I panicked, for a moment I felt like getting up and running away for a second time. But that was only for a short moment that went almost before it had come and I stood up, next to her, my head bent over hers, tears in my voice, I didn't dare even touch her, I kept saying "my love, my sweet love, what have I done to you, does it hurt, what have I done, forgive me my love, my sweet love, please forgive me" until her body suddenly relaxed, her face was lit up with a smile, she rested her head on my shoulder, "hold me so", and I put my arm round her shoulders and, softly, very very softly, trembling with love, I kissed her full mouth.

Even now I can remember the touch of her lips, the thrill and the joy. Love was oozing from my eyes, my ears, my mouth, the tips of my fingers. My skin was in love, my heart, my throat, all of me was in love. And her love came to me, I felt it piercing my body, hot smooth exciting. We never said a word. We were so close to each other that there was no room between us for words. My lips touched hers again, briefly, innocently. And then again, her neck, her forehead, her eyes

– "not the eyes, please, it means separation, don't you know? Here is my mouth kiss me" – and so her mouth again and the back of her ear – how did I think of it, where had I learnt it? and her hair, her thick long jet-black hair and – then the mouth again, the mouth. I didn't know how to kiss, our tongues never touched, only the lips. And yet our kiss was stronger than red wine, it went straight to our heads. She was mine, I was her lover, we were married, we were not married, we had children of our own, there were only the two of us, the Germans had gone, the War was over, we were in India, we were in Africa, in Spain, in Tibet, we had a nice little home, we had grown old and had grandchildren around us, we were sailing in a white sailing-boat, we had an aeroplane and we were flying low over the sea. I was in the War and I had been decorated for bravery and was coming home on leave and she was there waiting for me, I was a spy and had dropped by parachute in Germany to carry out a dangerous mission, I nearly finished the War on my own, there was no War, we were crossing the desert riding on camels, under the scorching sun, we were sailing in the White Nile in the perfumed evening, we were in Samarkand and in Kabul and in Benares... When I came back to my senses I was exhausted by all this activity, by all this happiness. I helped her climb down from the wall and, holding hands, we returned home riding on our cloud. And I was thinking that, no matter what was to come to me in later years, that morning I had already had as much happiness as a man has a right to have in a whole lifetime.

THERE FOLLOWED A WHOLE YEAR WHICH, IN THE GROWing misery and the fear and the humiliation of the Occupation, saw us grow up, live through situations that were not for us, gain a sort of wisdom much beyond our age, learn how to love in a way that was both fairy-tale and very much down to earth. All around us people died of hunger, people were betrayed and put to prison. People taken hostages by the Germans were executed in revenge for acts of the Resistance, others sold their bodies and their souls to save their skins. The Resistance grew and expanded and became organized in the mountains, spread into the towns, taking in men and women, young and old. And we lived the horror and the excitement that was the War, she and I, we lived those times with our own individual intensity, the fury of our love, the discovery of our life and our own selves. We used to come out of our homes in the night, secretly, after the curfew (men were shot for this by the German patrols) we stole out after everybody had gone to bed and we met in the open plot between the two houses, hidden by the bushes and the tall grass. A narrow little road was all that existed there, very few people moved around even in the daytime, no cars, so, of course, the danger was not all that great, even if a patrol happened to pass by they probably would not have seen us. Yet it was daring on our part and this added its own taste to our meetings, I felt particularly protective towards her and not a little heroic – there was magic in it all and it was intensely exciting. This is no exaggeration, the calmest moment in the War was bigger and more important than the most exciting time in peace.

And then the time came when somebody spoke to me and I joined the Resistance. No joke this even if I was a kid. I may have been only fifteen at the time and I may never have had the chance to do anything particularly difficult yet the little I had to do was far more important and dangerous than anything that children of the same age have to do to-day. You had the Germans to face then and if they caught you age was not a safeguard. So I joined the Movement and took part in secret meetings and went out during the nights, on missions, and left anti-German messages and pamphlets under the front doors of houses and in the streets and painted messages on walls – one night we were nearly caught by a patrol and had to run for our lives and we hid, my two comrades and myself, in the dug-out that Father had made in our garden during the war with Italy, the message on the wall of a neighbouring house left unfinished in the middle of a word, the last letter ending in a hurried brush stroke of paint – once I held an empty gun in my hands, only this made me feel revulsion rather than anything else, and on another occasion they told us how a grenade works though I never even saw one. All this when I was not fully fifteen and no small thing to me, my own tiny contribution to something meteoric and shattering, ugly and magnificent and utterly unique. Just to exist then, to live that period of history, was in itself heroic, to take active part in it gave it superhuman dimensions. And through all this our love. It grew and tied us close. I had told her about my involvement, I remember that I did not try to make it sound great, my true share was more than enough and so it was for her, her care and concern, the pride in her eyes, showed her feelings plainly and this was my reward, my medal. Every day brought something new and unexpected, a message or a rumour that stirred us and kept us alive. Even if nothing particular happened there was always the expectation and the waiting for what might happen – and that, too, was enough to keep us going. Most of the evenings, down in the neighbour's cellar, we listened to the news from London, on the radio he had kept hidden from the Germans there, we lived for that hour, needed it as a thirsty man needs water. The grown-ups talked solemnly and we listened in excitement to the rumours and the information, the truth and the lies, we had become experts in reading between the lines of the German war communiqués and thus knew when things went wrong for them and this gave us hope and strength to carry on living with the enemy amongst us, face to face with the ever-present Evil without being destroyed. Life was more inviting than at any other time.

WE CONTINUED TO PLAY IN THE GARDEN AND IN THE open plot with our friends, though now our play had a different quality to it because of our secret. Meaningful looks, surreptitious touching, quick pressing of the hands, all these and the thought that the others knew nothing of what we did, increased the excitement. But we were not so often with our friends now, we invented excuses to escape from them and go for long walks on our own or just sit some place by ourselves and talk for hours, or be silent together, just being together was already more important to us than any subject for conversation. We liked to go, the two of us, every morning to the baker's and there to wait in the queue for the pitiful portion of rationed bread – which often was not enough for all so everybody tried to be there two and three hours before the bakery opened, to queue and fight, in the cold of winter or in the heat of summer, all of us exhausted by malnutrition and the general suffering, queueing for hours, swearing or in silence, the grown-ups often trying to steal a place in the line from us children, a queue that was degrading and inhuman, taking from us our last bit of self-respect in order to give us something that was less than the minimum necessary to keep us alive, and we had to accept this because, above all, we must not die. This was now our personal account with Fate and we had to settle it in victory and not in defeat. And we liked it, where others were angry or evil or spiritless, we liked it just because it meant we could be together for two and three hours, side by side, holding hands, whispering in low conspiratorial voices, carrying our flowers when, all around us, the world was thundering and shaking and crumbling. And when the waiting was over, holding carefully our miserable pieces of bread, and those for the rest of our families, a so-called bread, made of corn and dirt and ground stones (once we found a bit of a mouse-tail in it), we returned home happy – and in this happiness the War lost all its might and fury. So we defeated the War every day. Because War is defeated when it does not exist in the hearts of men. In summertime there was one more queue in the hot early afternoon, when the very earth was baked in the sun, when we had to walk all the way to where ice was distributed, half a slab for each house, and there to wait for more than an hour to get our share. We looked forward to this, too, to the astonishment of our families; we took our net-bags and we started on our way as if we were going on a picnic. And this was even harder than the bread in the morning because, apart from the merciless heat, the ice was heavy, too heavy for our weakened arms, Gioconda could not manage on her own, so I carried mine in one hand and shared hers with the other, the two of us exhausted and sweating and happy, swinging the net-bag to and fro and watching the drops of water as they fell and formed a line on the ground which dried up immediately and vanished. Like promises... With fear and death around us, we hoped and dreamed. Our hearts were wide open to the misery and the sorrow, the nightmare of it all – but in the depth of our depths there remained an impregnable core of serene joy. There were many occasions when, in the middle of the night, we were awakened by shots in the streets. And some times, next morning there would be a man lying dead in the gutter. Then we looked on the ugly face of unfair death, shaking, sunk in deep sadness, unable to understand this monstrous irrationality. And then we tried to forget it by talking of the world as it would be after the War, a new world towards which we, too, would have contributed a little.

FOR A LONG PERIOD OF TIME WE WANTED NOTHING more than to be simply together, to go for a walk, to kiss in our clumsy way whenever we could. Our bodies had not awoken yet and made no demands. It is true that, for some time past, when I was on my own, I had started to have exciting fantasies that made me restless in my bed but when I was with Gioconda my body seemed not to know what it wanted. We continued meeting with the rest of our friends but even when we were with them we were somewhere else. Rudi had shyly reappeared and had been baffled by our warm reception of him. For us he was now the dearest of them all and we showed this openly and he was at a loss to understand it – but he never betrayed suspicion or malice. Nor did we ever tell him about us. We were proud of our love but we didn't want it to be known by the others, it was our precious secret.

AND SO THERE CAME A NIGHT WHEN I LAY IN MY BED and from the open window there entered into my room all those myriad noiseless sounds, that you feel rather than hear, of a peaceful night, such as only a night in the War can be, and I waited quietly for sleep to come but it didn't – and then I thought of her naked. And so I lost my sleep for good and I discovered my body. It was tense and vibrating and calling me with an urgent call. I held it in my hand, touched it with my fingers, I was trembling all over. An excitement and a confusion, I didn't know what I was doing. Everything was different this time. A huge, agonizing pleasure choked me, my heart was in my mouth. Her body was by my side, faintly white, her breasts were pressing my face and, after a long-drawn moment, wave upon wave rushed out from inside me, drenching my hand and my thighs and the bed-clothes. I lay on my back, exhausted with pleasure, paralysed with fear. I had no idea what had happened to me. I was convinced that what I had felt coming out of me must have been blood. I touched my legs and felt something sticky. I was so scared I didn't dare turn on the light, lest someone would notice it and come into my room, and I was trying to think what I would say to my mother the next morning when she saw the bloodstain. Then again, blood doesn't stick like that and, in the faint light of the room, I couldn't make out any stain, much as I screwed my eyes and peered closely. I was baffled. I had had my first solitary affair and it had caught me completely unprepared. I knew nothing about these things. Puberty had come to me during the War. Schools had been closed for over a year, so there was no contact with well-informed schoolmates. My friends were boys and girls younger than I was. We never talked about such things with Rudi. At that time, there were no books or magazines of an erotic kind, nor any films or even dirty photographs. There was a touching contradiction between what we knew and what we didn't. We were the innocent wise generation. Right in the thick of the War, and just because of it, we had learned the meaning of death and the struggle for survival – yet we had no idea how children were born. At fifteen, we knew less than children of eight to-day.

But I, at least, had that night made my discovery and, by God, it was great. Before I met her next morning I had done it – with "her" – two more times and, in the bathroom, in the plain light of day, I had studied it with roused curiosity, I had felt excited and proud at the sight of my potent manhood. And from that moment on I did it again and again, always with her in my mind, each time the same sweet explosive repetition of the same sweet explosive experience, accompanied by a rich variety of everchanging fantasies, according to how it suited my mood of the moment.

Next day, in the evening, choking with expectation, when darkness had fallen and our various friends had dispersed, I pulled her after me into a corner of the garden and pressed her with my body against the apricot-tree, and she responded simply by not withdrawing from my excitement, unconsciously ready, she only raised her eyes for a moment and looked at me and smiled shyly, in the half-light of the summer evening, her look a warm welcome and a promise for all that had been piling up inside us waiting for that moment. And then, suddenly, she moved imperceptibly and this was too much for me, more than I could hold back, she was really with me this time and not in my imagination, my spine emptied, an uncontrollable spasm shook me, my head was spinning, I was kissing her hair, my hand was squeezing her already ripe breast.

EVEN NOW I CAN REMEMBER THAT FANTASTIC PERIOD of my life, the awakening of the senses in a delirium of colours and emotions and desires and needs – and all the time there was the War and the duty to survive in a clear-cut and absolutely defined struggle that must erase the taste of defeat, when everything was black and white, no room for doubts and hesitation.

I was lost in the liquid expanse of her eyes with their timeless instinct wisdom and permanent invitation, the primitive knowledge of all those things that she had not yet learned and was impatient to know. Both of us impatient to know, to find out about ourselves through the heat of our bodies, the kaleidoscope of our senses, as if driven by a premonition that before long we would be called upon to pay our insignificant, colossal, due.

SOME TEN MONTHS PASSED SO. AND THEN, IN FEBRUARY of 1943, Théo died. He was a Belgian pianist, Professor of Music in the Conservatoire of Salonika, who lived in the ground floor of our house. His daughter Gigi, a pretty blonde, seven years older than I, who had a fine soprano voice, took lessons from a well-known lesbian music-teacher who came twice a week and usually overstayed her time. There was no music to be heard from downstairs for the last half hour or so; I, of course, never knew what it was all about and the whisperings and mutterings of my parents puzzled me. Théo's wife, Charlotte, was a shrew, and she and her mother Tante Lucie, an old hag full of life and wickedness, both treated Théo with contempt. Gigi was simply indifferent.

A charming man he was, the archetype of the true artist, wrapped up in his music, living in his own world. He studied on the piano every morning and evening, so I grew up literally feeding on classical music; the houses of that time were built so that only a wooden floor separated one storey from the other so all sounds penetrated easily and when he played the piano it was if he were playing in our own apartment but I visited downstairs too, as often as I could, he would let me sit in a corner of his room and listen to him playing – and, later, many were the times when Gioconda would come too and we sat there, awkward and still like wooden figures, timid and ecstatic, he was as good and kind to her as he was to me as he was to the whole world.

For as long as I remembered him, he used to drink heavily. And as time passed drink became for him more and more the substitute for the love that was lacking in his home and so the contempt of his wicked wife and her mother increased and they manipulated him any way they liked. I never learned why and how he came to live in our town; his room was full of medals and other tokens of recognition, of prizes he had won, when he had been young, in various cities of Europe. With the coming of the War, and then the Occupation, his downfall course started and from the autumn of 1942 he never even left home. He only rarely studied the piano then; most of the time he lay on the narrow sofa, in the music-room, which served him as a bed as well. He was like those plants that are made to live in warm climates yet his life was a perpetual winter. I loved him dearly and so did my parents and so did all the neighbours, but this wasn't enough.

His end was a suitable finale to a life that, for much too long, had lost all trace of humanity. He had been losing weight steadily, receiving no care from his family except the miserable meals which his wife prepared reluctantly and which she served with hatred. And which he ate alone in his room. I don't know what his illness was. Maybe it was a combination of his chronic alcoholism and the malnutrition that we all suffered from because of the Occupation. But, above all, it must have been the despair of his heart, with which he had lived for much longer than anyone would have endured, the final defeat and the capitulation.

We talked about him often, Gioconda and I; we tried to think of what we could do to help him, knowing that nothing could help him, we could do nothing but love him and feel sad about him as we listened to him playing the piano, seated together in his room or out in the garden, holding hands.

AND THERE CAME THAT EVENING, A VERY COLD AND clear evening, in the middle of February, when it had been snowing for two days and then the weather had cleared and the stars were pushing each other for a place in the sky and the snow had frozen on the branches of the trees and on the dry flower-pots and on the fence around the garden and on the ground, so that everything looked like a delayed Christmas toy for the children of a giant.

On that evening, Gigi had decided to give a party. For quite some time now she had been mixing with the Germans, and her guests on that evening were three German officers and two Greek girls who arrived around seven bringing bottles of wine and parcels of food and sweets – things that we hadn't tasted for more than two years and for which there were many who had sold their bodies and even their souls to taste once and to remember. We heard them when they came and we saw them from behind the closed shutters of our windows, the officers tall and handsome and bursting with health but clumsy too and awkward in their attempt to appear at ease. The girls, pretty and very young, trying to look as if they were doing nothing wrong, as if they did not care whether people despised them, but failing to convince and looking rather pitiable under the burden of their guilt.

The gramophone started playing almost at once and the German songs could be heard very clearly through the wooden floor. All those nice little songs, the popular successes that, before the War, had brought gaiety to our homes, the grown-ups dancing to their tune when friends were visiting in the evenings, we, the children, crowded together in our corner, happy, watching them, thinking of when we would be old enough to dance like them. Father liked those songs, he played them on the gramophone on Sunday mornings and then he would lift me up on his shoulders and would dance around the room, I just old enough to be able to feel proud and very very happy. All those songs – *Eine Nacht in Monte-Carlo*, and *Eine Kleine Konditorei* and *Das ist die Liebe der Matrosen*, nothing was nicer and more nostalgic than those German songs – and now, this evening, we had to listen to them again and we went mad to have to confess that we liked them when all we wanted was every scrap of an excuse to hate the Germans and everything that was theirs. Soon, all of them started singing together downstairs, accompanying the music, the officers' voices strong and masculine, Gigi's sweet and clear. They were in the corner room which was the sitting-room, separated by a large hall from Théo's music-room. Gigi's mother and her grandmother used the room in the rear where they always retired very discreetly when Gigi was entertaining her friends at home.

It was easy to tell that the party downstairs was a success because of the increasing level of noise and the disorder, together with the declining quality of the singing. Towards midnight it had become a mere cacophony of hysterical girlish screeches, coarse Germanic guffaws, the sound of glasses thrown against the wall and, every now and then, brief, obscene, silences. And then, sudden and horrible amidst this nightmare, was heard the voice of Théo calling: "Gigi, Gigi". The noise downstairs continued unchanged. The cry was heard again after a while and then again and again. It was a desperate call of grave need and distress that pierced our stomachs. The singing stopped for a brief moment but, immediately after, another glass was broken against the wall and a hoarse drunken voice started a new song, out of tune now, a well-known military march. The others took it up and soon we heard the heavy rhythm of army boots going round and round the room below, shaking the whole house. The Aryans downstairs had started a proper parade, for all we knew they might be goose-stepping too. So now there was no inconsistency whatever between the quality of the noise and the concept we had about everything Germanic, no mistake about the origin and the nationality. I saw a change come over Father's face, something imperceptible and undefinable, which not only Mother, who could anyway read his face even in the dark, but which I too understood and we knew that he had made his decision and that nothing we did would stop him now because this was now beyond all control of reason or even fear and not only for him but for us too, for Mother who under any other circumstances would know how to talk to him and for me who would like to go with him only I knew that this would not do and Mother knew this too, we both knew that he had to go alone and we had to stay upstairs, trying to hear everything that went on below, the slightest sound, and understand its meaning correctly, hoping, praying, that neither he nor the Germans would do anything that must not be done, knowing that it would not take longer than a few minutes only how does one stand these minutes.

Of what followed, a little we were able to guess while it was happening, the rest we just hoped and prayed for or simply refused to fear it. When Father eventually came back upstairs, his face empty of blood and the expression in his eyes not human and after he had had time to stop shaking and to start thinking again and to speak coherently, only then were we able to really grasp what had taken place below, only then could we accept that such a thing could have happened and that he, Father, had seen and had lived it all.

When he had made his decision to go to them, knowing that neither Mother nor I would try to stop him, he left the room quickly and silently, went down the inner stairs, out of the door and down the outer stairs, into the garden and into the clear frozen night, wearing only his sweater, no overcoat and no hat, nothing to protect him from the bitter cold except his anger and his blind determination. He stood outside the front door of the ground floor and knocked. And before they could have the time to answer him he knocked again and again. And as he stood there, he heard Théo calling Gigi again and he heard the noise of the party going on as if nothing was happening and so he started banging on the door with all his force, without stopping, determined, as he said later, not to stop until they opened or until he had broken the door or his hands, we upstairs hearing the banging and our pulse beating together with it, only now the fear could not reach our minds because there was as much anger and hatred in us now as in the knocking below.

Eventually they heard him or decided to pay attention to him or, simply, became fed up with him and so the music stopped and we upstairs heard the door of their room open and the heavy steps going towards the front door and then we heard the door open and then there followed a few moments of utter silence when we did not think of anything, could not think of anything, we only stood there, Mother and I, bent and not moving, trying to hear and terrified not only of what we might hear but also of what we might not hear. Father told us afterwards that, when he heard them coming towards the front door, he felt suddenly very calm and in control of himself, a thick layer of cold-bloodedness over his seething rage. In front of him stood, when the door opened, one of the officers and, a couple of steps behind, Gigi. What was unexpected and, in a strange way, Father said, nauseating, was that both of them were properly dressed and calm, as if all this time they had done nothing but hold a serious conversation. Beyond the fact that the officer was wearing no tie, there was nothing else wrong with his appearance. Nor was there anything to object to in the simple attractive appearance of Gigi, dressed as she was in a plain woollen dress. Even the fact that her lips had no lipstick on them did not seem to indicate that this was so because she had been kissing. Father said that all this made him angrier than if he had found them naked and making love. But when he spoke to them, all that he had been expecting was there all right. Their dull expression, the near imbecile indifference to what was happening, a tendency in Gigi to start giggling, all this was there and it was not easy at all for Father to bear.

They had opened the door and had been standing there, looking at him almost as if they had been expecting him yet without inviting him in, just standing there and looking at him, saying nothing, only Gigi looking as if she might start giggling at any moment and Father trying to keep calm, knowing that if he lost his self-control he would either start screaming or he would be sick, when Théo cried her name again, three times in succession. "I think he is going to die," Father said to Gigi. "I think that he is trying to tell you this, that he wants you near him when he dies. It is terrible to die alone."

"Yes," said Gigi. She did not move.

"What is he telling you?" the officer asked her in German.

"I think he is going to die," Father told him in German. "I think that he is trying to tell her that and that he wants her near him when he dies. It is terrible to die alone."

"Yes," said the officer. He did not move.

It was mad, Father said, beyond all reality. It was beyond anything that he had been prepared for, ready to fight against. And then, as they stood so, the two of them indifferent and remote, almost politely patient, he, Father, trying to control his mind and keep in touch with sanity, trying to survive, then, from Théo's room the piano was heard playing. For the first time Father saw them react. Nothing specific, a fleeting change – but it had been there. For a fraction of a moment they stiffened, froze, an expression of fright passed over their face. Father used to say afterwards that that moment was sufficient for their punishment, that justice had been done.

Théo was playing the Adagio from the *Moonlight Sonata*. It had always been one of his favourite pieces. The sound came to us very soft, very sad. It spoke of a dream of superhuman dimensions that had often seemed on the point of realization but had slipped away at the last moment. He was playing it, this time, a little more slowly than usual, yet, listening to it then, one felt that that's how it should always be played, never any different.

We heard it upstairs and, after a moment of stupefaction, a crazy relief came over us, our bodies relaxed, we felt hopeful that, after all, everything was all right. But this lasted very briefly, the next moment we knew that something extraordinary must be happening below, the unusual way the piano was played, the absolute silence from everybody downstairs, all this finally brought us the message – and the horror of it was stamped on our minds. The three of them below had turned to stone while the piano was heard, the others in the room must have felt the same, no sound came from their room, no sound from the back room either, no sound from all the earth, only this unnatural music from behind the closed door of the dying man, the sound of his soul that spread and rolled and penetrated everywhere, our bodies and our blood and our mind, and we were all turned into pieces of frozen anticipation. It faded away and soared up again, infinitely beautiful, until it reached its end. There followed a silence for a few moments, complete silence – then a terrible prolonged cry that seemed as if it would never end. And then nothing. A final definitive nothing which could be followed by nothing and which left no room for doubt or waiting. Father rushed into the room. Théo was leaning backwards in the chair in front of the piano, his face towards the ceiling. His eyes were closed, Father said, in a last act of mercy from God and the expression on his face, after that last cry of protest, was almost serene. Father left the room and went out of the house and into the garden. Gigi and the officer had not moved.

THE MONTHS WENT BY. OUR LOVE HAD TAKEN ON A NEW dimension which meant that we could not now enjoy ourselves as easily as before, nor could we continue with our old habits and be the same with our friends. Now we wanted, needed, more than at any time before, to be alone, hidden away from the eyes of the world. We needed the dark. Only this could hide our caresses which had no roof to cover them.

While summer lasted it was daytime practically till curfew time. Slipping out of our houses after that had been forbidden by our parents for some time now, when they had found out we had been doing it, even though they had never asked us any awkward questions. Too many people had paid a heavy penalty for ignoring the curfew and venturing outdoors and so our parents had to be very strict about it. On the other hand, summer had its advantages – one could sit anywhere, we could lie on the dry grass or stretch on the beach. We became very cautious and conspiratorial. Often we must have given cause to our friends to regard our behaviour with wonder, if not actual suspicion, and I frequently thought that I had caught them looking at me in a strange manner – but it may have been my guilty imagination.

Within a short while we had discovered all the right places, everywhere where we could hide, in our neighbourhood and a little beyond. Open deserted plots, where the grass grew high and where there were bushes (often with thorns that pricked us) or low walls and fences around neglected gardens, tall trees with big trunks. We discovered an old hut, in the middle of a large open area of deserted land (it is difficult to realize now how much free space there existed then in a town like Salonika), a hut that was decrepit and ready to fall, nobody lived in it any more, the door would not close properly. Inside, there were piles of rubbish, old objects rotting away, there was even animal dung – and sometimes human too – and frequently it smelled bad. And yet we regarded this hut as our biggest find. We had a roof over our heads at last. Smells or no smells, litter or dung, who cared about such things then. Our love was very tolerant. A dark corner was often enough – even in the rain and the cold of the winter, let alone a place with a roof on it. We were very lucky to have found it. There was also a sweet mongrel dog that used to live there; we became great friends with him, especially after I had brought him some stale food once, he was very useful to us too when we were inside because he would growl angrily as soon as someone would appear anywhere near and so we had plenty of time to arrange ourselves properly. Otherwise he would be just friendly, lying on the ground and patting it with his tail to show us that he liked us to be there with him. Of course there was no room where we could lie down in there, not even where we could sit. Whatever we did we had to do it standing, almost always in a hurry and with the fear that someone might come, a drunk or a bad man. But we didn't mind all that much. This was our shelter and we enjoyed the illusion of security it offered us. In those years of the War and the Occupation, we had all learned how not to ask for much. We had learned how to live, and be content, with the bare essentials whether it was food or clothing or recreation. Or anything else. Within our narrow limits we had developed a new system of values, with its own proportions, so that even the smallest event took on a new significance. Ersatz coffee, made of some sort of dry beans, a jacket made by sewing together bits of cloth and flannel, a book lent by a friend, anything that we did not expect – and we had learned not to expect anything – gave a new intense colour to our lives and brought us joy that could last for days. So it was with our love. Those secretive hurried uncomfortable meetings never lasted for more than half-an-hour, at the most. But within that short time were concentrated the pleasure and the emotion, the passion, of hours and days, food and substance which, unbeknown to us still, would serve to fill the void that she would leave behind when she was gone for ever. I remember those hours with deep gratitude and I pray to God that the nightmare which must have been the last months of her life, may have been softened a little, lost some of its horror, with their memory, with the fullness of our life those last wonderful terrible months. I shall never know.

SHE HAD AN INSATIABLE NEED TO TAKE AND TO GIVE, with heart and body, while she remained irresistibly innocent.

When we had reached, almost running, panting, our own chosen corner or our tree or we had disappeared into the old hut and had fixed the door from inside with a plank so that it could not be opened easily from outside, she would grab my head with both her hands and our mouths would seek each other almost angrily, our bodies pressed below the waist, small imperceptible movements full of lust that would make us faint. And we would start touching each other, almost aggressively, searching, I would lift her dress up with impatient shaking hands, she would undo the buttons of my trousers, sometimes breaking them. This first contact would finish me almost always before she had had time to free my body from my clothes – just to feel her hand sliding downwards was enough for me to see red and lose all control. She had come to accept this and was even amused by it and used to tease me. Immediately afterwards, however, it was her turn and this was terribly important for me, an intense need to feel her excitement, her fulfillment complementing mine, and I to know that I was the cause of it. So when I had calmed down and rested for a few moments (those unique moments following my own excitement, when all my strength had poured out from inside me and I was like a little child, powerless, she could have done to me whatever she chose, she could even have killed me and I would not have resisted and yet what she did, with that instinctive wisdom which she possessed, was to hold my head and stroke it softly, kissing my neck my cheeks my forehead and "come love, come, here now, easy, here love, all right darling, I love you, easy, easy," kissing me, stroking my head, sweetly and tenderly, while my spasms receded and I relaxed and offered myself up to her power and her protection) and I was ready and feeling man again, eager to give her now what it was her right to expect from me, I pressed her against me with an almost aggressive embrace which she understood, she knew what it meant and so she responded eagerly, she now the child in my hands and the woman and the lover, devoured by her own passion.

SHE KNEW HOW TO ENJOY HERSELF AND SHE HAD A FINE sense of humour which helped her pick out the funny details of everyday life and then her laughter sounded fresh and lively. Yet at the same time she displayed occasional, inexplicable moments of deep consternation. She could become suddenly very serious. Like a cloud that, blown by the wind, covers the sun for a few moments and its darkness brings fear, then it is light again, so did her face become grave at times, her eyes seemed to be looking beyond me at something which I could not see, a sort of sadness covered her face.

This frightened me terribly when it happened and I would pull her towards me then and plead with her to tell me. But she would only shake her head, she would squeeze her body on mine, then, just as suddenly, she would come out of this mood, she would give me a quick kiss, she would laugh – and it would be sunshine again, it would be warm, there would be no War, no fear, only love, love everywhere.

What very few people find in a whole lifetime, yet everybody is searching for all the time, had been given me, a special favour, in the beginning of my life. And I think now that I have never stopped trying to find her again in every woman that I have had ever since. Maybe that's why the endless search, the myriad new faces, maybe that's why the loneliness.

There were moments when (as we hid in the hut or leant against the big tree or sat on the low wall, listening to the tail of the dog patting happily on the ground or to the sound of the sea or to the wind, her skirt pulled up and my body wedged between her legs or held in her hands that now knew how to caress in the manner of a very experienced woman, our mouths kissing wildly, our tongues fighting each other, my fingers exploring her under her clothes, both of us almost cannibalistic in our devouring need for each other, shaking, panting, until we came again and then again, both of us now, simultaneously, a mad sharing of pleasure, the final communication, the very substance of our bodies) I felt the physical limits of my self dissolve and expand and surround her, to absorb her as the amoeba takes in its food, I felt as if I were taking her completely inside me, turning her into one with me – and thus making her finally and irrevocably mine.

I sometimes fear that the moment may come when my mind will begin to forget the details. This thought frightens me endlessly. I want to hold in my memory everything that has happened to us and between us, every small moment, every time she said "I love you," every time she touched me in that particular manner that she alone knew by her instinct. To remember always her voice when she whispered words to me, the touch of her lips, the smell of her body. To remember not only all that was said between us but all our silences, too. People die only when we forget them. She must stay alive as long as I live – and then beyond me. Alive as I knew her, as she blossomed under my very eyes, my caresses, my kisses.

STRANGE AS IT MAY NOW SEEM, IN SPITE OF THE INTENsity of our love, we hadn't even thought, for a long time, of making love properly. We didn't need this to show to each other how we felt and, I think, at that phase of our affair it would probably have been very difficult for a more complete form of love to increase the pleasure and the satisfaction which a mere touch of our bodies gave us. So we didn't need it physically either. Our bodies were too full of animalistic force, were too much in a hurry to have the need or the time for luxuries. A simple gesture, a touch, were enough to break the dam open and let go a hot flood. We never thought of complaining of our lot or to ask for more – all we wanted was somewhere where we could be left alone for half-an-hour.

So, when it did happen, it came by itself; we were unprepared for it, consciously at least. There came an afternoon when my parents left home very early to pay a visit to some relatives who lived across the town. Public transport being what it was in those times, they needed about an hour to go and as much to come back. They wouldn't stay there less than two hours, so the house would be empty and free for at least four hours. I became aware of all this only when my parents had left and I was alone in the house. When I heard the garden gate close behind them, I realized, very suddenly and very vividly, that I had the house all to myself to do as I pleased. There had been other times in the past, of course, when I had stayed alone. But, on those occasions, my only thought had been to go out and seek her and take her for a walk which would end at one of our usual hideouts. I had never thought until then, nor had she, to use the house. But this time, quite inexplicably, it was different. So maybe I was unconsciously ready for it. The only thing I knew, when I found myself alone that day, was that I wanted her very much to be with me there. No thoughts about what would happen next, I had no idea whatsoever, I might even have been scared if anybody had been able to foretell. Just for her to be there with me was so exciting that I had great difficulty in putting on my trousers. I managed to get dressed eventually and I went out to seek her. It was very early in the afternoon, nobody was around in the heat of that summer day, no passers-by All the houses had their shutters closed, hers too. Nothing can be as quiet and still now as were those hours in the War. Our neighbourhood which, in those days, consisted of pretty tidy little houses, each with its own garden, of open spaces where the grass grew high in the summer and where we could play unmolested to our heart's content, trees and flowers everywhere, has been transformed now into one of the ugliest parts of Salonika, noisy and dirty. The smallest piece of land has been built upon; big, cheap, tasteless blocks of flats have sprouted everywhere and look decrepit as soon as they have been built. Of poor construction, colourless – or with loud misfitting colours – the paint starting to peel off even before it has dried, the doors and windows badly fitting, the small useless balconies crammed with pieces of old furniture together with the big barrels that hold oil for the oil-stoves, wires stretching across to hang the washing, not one garden anywhere, not one tree or flower, a wasteland inhabited by wasted human beings. The friendly middle-class families that had lived there for decades have now gone and their place has been taken over by a noisy crowd of hundreds of low-class households, coarse people constantly bickering with each other, people who came from their villages to make their fortune in the big city and who can't go back now nor feel at home here. The children have nowhere to play, nothing but narrow pavements and sunless streets thick with noisy old smelly cars. And there are dozens of these poor children now where there were only a handful of us then. And there is the noise and clamour of Peace now where there was the peace and quiet of the War then.

So, on that hot afternoon all was quiet and still when I went out to find her and the sun beat down on my excitement and the silence sang songs in my heart.

I stood undecided in the open lot between our two houses, not knowing what to do, impatient, already fearing that she might not come out and thus the opportunity be lost. Up to that moment, in my hurry, I had not thought that I might not find her or that she might not want to come with me to the house. Now, as I stood there lost, this thought crossed my mind and I felt sick, expectation and desire and fear turned my knees to jelly. All this did not last long, however; I can't have stayed there for more than a couple of minutes when I saw the front door of their house open quietly, cautiously, and she came out, came to me, in controlled haste, and nodded to me without a word and led me to the back of their house, away from the windows of her parents' bedroom, away from indiscreet eyes. Between that side of the house and the high wall of the neighbour's garden there was a narrow passage that led to the kitchen door where, of course, there was nobody at that time. She had a cheap dress on, the material was clinging to her body; it was already too tight and short for her – the way she was growing – at the front where there was a row of buttons from the neck down to her waist, the two halves stretched against the buttons as they were pushed out by her full breasts, her bare skin showing in between.

"How did you know I was out? Weren't you asleep?" I asked her in a whisper. "No, I wasn't asleep. It's a long time since I have been able to sleep in the afternoons." She smiled. "Can you sleep in the afternoons?" she added with a twinkle in her eyes. And she went on before I could say a word. "I often sit behind the shutters and I look through them at your house, your garden, I think of you, of us, of a lot of things."

She spoke in a whisper too, playing absently with the collar of my shirt. I nearly grabbed her there, on the spot. I was aroused and she could see it but she did nothing this time, no gesture, so she must have known what I had in mind for that day.

"I saw your parents go so I sat and waited. I knew you would come." "And do you know why I have come to-day?" "No, I don't," her voice was barely heard, "but I have thought of something..." "I think we must both have thought of the same thing. Come on, let's go." Everything continued to be deserted all around, yet my heartbeat had gone crazy. I was already filled with an exquisite sense of impending sin – and I am sure the same was true for her. Even after we reached home safely and we went into my room, we were very cautious and we took off our shoes and walked about on tiptoe, lest Gigi or her Mother below had seen my parents go and now heard two people moving around and suspected something. Not that we were about for long, she just asked to see the whole house – "I only know your living-room, I now want to see it all, so I can think of you anywhere here when I am at home alone." When we returned to my room, she stood in front of the book-case and read carefully the titles of all the books there, then she went and stood looking at the large photograph of my Father, on the wall above the old desk, she looked at him for a long time, Father young, around thirty, stiff collar and bow-tie and a pointed moustache. There, under his smiling eyes, I stood behind her, my body pressing hers fiercely, I put my arms over her shoulders, slid my hands inside her dress and inside the tight bra – and felt dizzy when she pulled in her chest to help my hands – and I touched her nipples that had grown hard and were sticking out, well-made and already dark coloured, impatient under my fingers. She bent her head backwards onto my shoulder, a sigh left her half-closed lips, her eyes misted over, her hands gripped mine outside her dress. And then she moved her body just so, quite imperceptibly, with a knowledge worthy of an experienced woman, so as to fit mine more conveniently, and this, not the gesture so much as the intention behind the gesture, was enough for me, I felt it coming inside me like a river swollen by rain, I almost heard the roaring. I just had time to step back and free my body and the spasms came, almost painful, drenching my handkerchief and my hands and her hands as she turned too, like she was spring-loaded, and was now holding me there with both her hands, her eyes closed now, her breathing heavy, the words coming out sharp and short, like the rhythm of my joy, "my love, my dearest, I love you, come love, my dearest, easy my love, love, love."

When I came back from the bathroom she was sitting on the divan, that served me as a bed for the night, her legs tucked away under her, her arms crossed on her lap, looking at Father's picture opposite. I sat beside her and pulled her lightly towards me. She settled against me, sighed with pleasure. The afternoon breeze was coming now from the sea through the closed shutters. "It's so nice here now," she murmured. "Cool, quiet. As if there is no War, nothing." "There is no War, love, not here, not this moment. War is so far away. War has got nothing to do with our love."

She sighed deeply and squeezed against me. She took my hand, brought it to her lips. I really don't know how much closer to happiness one can come. There can't have passed even half-an-hour from the moment we had come but it was as if she belonged already to my room, as if she were a part of my life in there, as if I actually remembered her there. Everything that I had imagined, all my fantasies about us, in the long hours that I had spent alone in my room, when I had wanted her and had not had her and I had to create her and set her next to me, all this seemed now as if it had really been, as if I had really lived it with her and not in my mind alone. It seemed impossible now that she had never been there before, alive and real, so I could talk to her and touch her and love her. For a moment I felt as if it was I who, until then, had not been real there and had now, at last, acquired a presence there. It was as if, until that moment, I had been but the phantom of my own desires, a premonition of my existence and I had materialized, I had become substance and truth the moment she had entered my room. She a vision in there up to then, a remorseless haunting figure that floated about filling the room and dominating it – and then leaving a void behind her and a need. And now she was there herself and from the moment she had come in it was as if she had always been there and to-day's coming was nothing but the confirmation of her pre-existence there. More than that, the extension and the continuation of my own self and of my own life. As I held her against me tightly, I had that sensation again which had haunted me before, only now much more vivid, that we had merged physically too, the tangible boundaries of our bodies had been dissolved and remade as one. A very intense momentary sensation of complete union accompanied by a sharp knowledge of the smallest detail around us and inside us and in all the world. Gradually, imperceptibly, we began to come alive. A little touch of a fingertip, a small pressure of one leg against another, a fleeting caress, an indefinable series of tiny signals that sent their message. She turned her face towards me and I took it in my hands, held it, I kissed her mouth greedily, impatiently, our tongues chasing each other. I was kissing her all over her face now, while my hands were trying, blindly, to undo the buttons of her dress, pulling it down her shoulders and my mouth was sliding downwards too and I lifted her arms and kissed her there, in the armpits that were wet with perspiration and had their own smell and their own taste and this was welcome too and exciting. I held my mouth there while my hands were fighting to undo her bra but my hurry was making me even more clumsy and I was getting nowhere until, with one quick dexterous movement, she got rid of it before I knew what she was doing – and this, her eagerness and her participation more arousing even than her naked breasts – and then put her arms round my waist and bent backwards to give me room to move, her breasts there in front of my eyes, expectant, I bent my head and pressed it between them and then started searching around, licking, I found her nipples, dark and ready, and played with them, torturing them, holding them in my mouth and then pulling back again to look at her, kissing her mouth again and her neck and behind the ears and the shoulders and the armpits and then the breasts again, those mature erotic breasts.

She pulled suddenly away from me and stood up, in front of me, and she reached with her hands and pulled me up towards her and we stood there looking at each other for a little while and we both knew now what we wanted to do next and so I pulled her dress all the way down and it fell around her feet and she just stepped out of it and stood again, motionless, looking me straight in the eyes, not a word, her silence more eloquent than speech, waiting, eager for my next move and I took off my shirt and, after a small moment of hesitation, I undressed completely and stood there still and hard and proud and she looked at it and then into my eyes again, a promise in her look, it was her turn again and she didn't hesitate at all but with a slow deliberate gesture she pulled down her last little garment, took it off, threw it aside and then let her arms fall by her sides and stopped there, unique in her nakedness, which I was seeing for the first time in its entirety, as I was showing mine for the first time to her and we were not ashamed at all, we were looking at each other, hungrily, from top to bottom, curious eager greedy, not only not shy but proud of our beauty and our strength, proud of our very desire itself. Then she made the first imperceptible movement towards me and the next moment we were holding each other tight, my hands searching her all over, her back her breasts her legs, pressing her with my body wedged between her thighs, rubbing against the thick curly hair with short, swift, strokes, which she returned with unexpected skill, an exquisite sense of rhythm, holding me with both her arms around my waist, her face on my shoulder, kissing me, half-biting me, rubbing her breasts against my chest with a slow circular voluptuous motion until it was almost painful to endure it and yet a torture that I would give anything to have to suffer all day long.

"Come, let us sit down," her voice almost fading, "it is too much, unbearably much. God, how much I love you..." We did not just sit down, we literally fell upon the sofa, as if a huge wave had thrown us there. We stretched and curled and turned and pressed and parted, so as to be able to look at each other, and grabbed and kissed, arms hands fingertips lips tongues teeth eyes, an interminable frenzied union, an exquisite confusion of inventiveness, an almost desperate, devouring, need not merely to have each other but to engulf and assimilate. She proved imaginative and had a glorious ability to understand before-hand my next move and to adapt eagerly. She was born for love. She knew instinctively how to receive and how to give and how to be herself, easy, without false modesty and all those no's and don't's, without guilt or self-reproach, straightforward with herself and honest in her love-making, with that innate ability for joy that made her able to give totally and spontaneously.

When we first kissed each other down there it

happened quite by chance, no premeditation whatsoever, the knowledge did not pre-exist. Very simply, there came a moment when, as we played with each other and stretched and spread and twisted, she got hold of my head between her legs, my face was suddenly buried in the thick hair, my mouth touched her. The very odour of her body and her sweat hit me like an aphrodisiac, my tongue started unconsciously to search, I played with my mouth, I kissed, I pretended to bite, and I felt the mounting of her pleasure, she bent her knees upwards; she trapped my head tightly between her thighs, pressing it with her hand on her body there, the muscles of her belly tightened, a groan came from deep inside her, she shook and twisted and squirmed like a fish thrown out of the water. And, in her turn, she discovered what she could do with her mouth and I suddenly felt my body surrounded by lips, tongue, teeth, she kissing it, playing with it, as it thrusted in the wet softness of her mouth, my mind turned inside out, my heart ached, my whole body hardened, I lost all sense of reality, all the self-control that I had miraculously maintained until then vanished like smoke blown away by a gust of wind and, before I had time to even think of withdrawing, I flooded her. Only for a moment did she stop and then she started again kissing, filling her mouth, swallowing, her incredible instinct of a woman helping her to overcome what, for her, must have been an unknown frightening and totally unexpected experience, not only to overcome it but obviously to enjoy this too, beyond any doubt enjoying it since, soon after, she came again herself, explosively, in a manner the like of which I had never before seen in her, an endless series of spasms that seemed as if they would never end until they began to grow less violent, short movements now that finally stopped altogether, leaving us both totally exhausted, our breathing deep now and slow, our faces still there in the same place, neither of us really knowing what had happened to us.

She whispered my name and I moved round and stretched alongside her, side by side, on our backs and then we turned towards each other so that we were face to face now, I looking at her mouth, that mouth which for me, from now on, would never be the same again. I took her face in my hands and I kissed her, the strange taste of my own substance on her lips. I wondered what she must have felt and thought. I was worried.

"Angry?" I asked her, kissing her again.

"Angry?" She laughed. "Angry? That's a good one. You are being stupid, aren't you?" Teasingly. "Angry for what? For what happened? Darling, this was part of you, I took you inside me, I have you in me now, I have you, I will walk around carrying you inside me. And if you want to know I will not even eat or drink anything for as long as I can to-day so as to keep your taste in my mouth. Love, oh my love, how much I really owe you."

We relaxed, submerged in an almost tangible joy that covered us like a protective cloak. We touched and our hands touched pleasure, we kissed and our mouths kissed pleasure. Lying side by side, our eyes closed now, our bodies barely touching, it felt as if we had been there for hours, every minute an experience of life condensed.

When finally I dared look at the clock I nearly shouted with joy, it was only just over an hour since we had come to the house, so we had as much, and more, before we would have to leave. I told her and she laughed with pleasure and she held me and kissed me and then she got up, passing over my body, and said she would leave me alone for a little to go to the bathroom and I said that I would go with her, that I wouldn't let her from my sight even a single moment and she laughed and said that this was forbidden and she ran and managed to lock the door behind her and I was left outside, banging on the door and crying that this was unfair and she laughing and I missing her, until she opened the door with a deep curtsey of mock obedience, her lovely face full of laughter, and she said that now I could go in but first to promise that I would let her wash her face and I said that I too wanted to wash my face, to cool myself, so we stood side by side, fighting to catch the soap from each other's hands, pushing, playing.

She finished first and ran back to the room and when I joined her she was sitting on the sofa, her legs bent up and tight together, her arms around them and her chin resting on her knees, looking at the door, so when I entered the room what I could see were her long legs and on top of them her smiling face with its mischievous look, a perfect picture of what she was, sweet and sensuous and loving, the gift of the gods to me and the dream that I did not know then how soon it would become a nightmare.

I stood there at the door and she smiled at me and then she looked down there where I was now small and without strength but, even so, important to her who loved that part of myself with a mixture of awe and curiosity and need so that, looking at me there, her eyes had a serious and far-away look that told me that this would never be anything but sacred to her, something about which she could talk only in a whisper. Now she knew that this would offer her the most exciting experience of her life and it was obvious to me that she looked at it as the first men on earth must have looked at fire, in the beginning of Life.

I went to the window and breathed in the fragrance of flowers that came from the garden. She rose quietly from the sofa and came and leaned next to me. We looked out from behind the half-drawn shutters, at the sunlit world, our ears buzzing with the song of the cicadas. Everything was in a haze, no one was stirring, nothing.

She was the first to hear the familiar crackling of the anti-aircraft guns far away.

"Listen listen," she whispered, excited, "they are coming again." Very soon the drone of the planes reached us from high up there, filling the afternoon quiet, getting steadily louder, ruthless and menacing, irrevocable like the punishment of God. Our hearts leapt in our breasts, I made as if to open the shutters. She caught my hand and stopped me.

"Darling, we are stark naked. Do you want somebody to see us?" So, we pressed tight against each other, trying to see out from the narrow opening between the two halves of the drawn-to shutters. The drone was now heard directly overhead and we could see the white puffs of the anti-aircraft against the hazy blue of the sky, as they tried, desperately and in vain, to stop the progress of those demonic machines up there.

The Allies had started their air-raids over a few months before, very rarely to be true, too infrequently for our impatient expectations, perhaps once a month, hitting usually the airfield. They used to come during the day but once they had come during the night and had bombed the harbour and had started some glorious big fires in the warehouses which the Germans used to store various war material in. I remember that night well – Mother terrified as usual, had run to hide in the dug-out which we had built, with great care, in our garden during the war with the Italians. (It was a fine construction, all lined inside with thick planks, wooden benches along the walls that could seat up to ten people, a thick wooden roof, on top of which a strong layer of corrugated iron offered further protection from shrapnel and debris, and on top of that again all the soil that had been excavated, forming a lovely rising where grass and camomile had grown. Inside there was a paraffin-lamp and garden tools to help us dig ourselves out in case a near-by fallen bomb would block the exit. It was there that we used to find shelter during the war with Italy, when the enemy planes came over and bombed Salonika, all of us, and Gigi and her parents and her grandmother, and almost always a friend or neighbour as well, each in his own accustomed place, Mother in the farthest corner always the first to arrive there running and panting, even before the first wail of the sirens had ended – where did she find such agility and speed of movement? – never forgetting to carry with her her bag with her jewels, in case the house was bombed, always crying out, as she fled, "Let us close the shutters and open the window," we teasing her for the use of the first person plural, perhaps that's how she deceived herself that she did participate.) So Mother had gone straight to the dug-out that memorable night while Father and I stood out in the balcony, looking transfixed at the grand spectacle. I can still remember now my intense excitement, it was the first time since the Germans had entered Salonika that they were at the receiving end just in front of our own eyes. I felt as if I was myself up there, one of the crew of those bombers, which we could hear though we could not see, I hitting the enemy down here with all the hatred and the need for revenge that I had learned how to carry in my young heart and which had been piling up for so long inside me without finding the outlet it needed. What I had done with my participation, at that age, in the Resistance (more than enough for a young boy to be sure, and for me almost heroic) was at this moment shrinking to its realistic dimensions as I stood, dazed, and witnessed that fury from the sky that night which shook my whole being and which gave vent, through the deeds of those airmen up there – who, of course, completely ignored my existence – to all my pent-up feelings; I worshipped them, yes, as the fires were rising up skywards, illuminating not only the harbour and the area around but our hearts too and the sky already multicoloured from the huge flares that descended slowly in their parachutes, dropped from the planes, everything like a splendid ruthless act of triumph; and the bombs dropping and exploding and shaking the earth, putting fire to the harbour and lighting another one in our hearts.

I was thinking of that night now, as we stood naked, pressing side by side behind the half-closed shutters, as we tried to see the planes, arms around our waists, tense and impatient. The only thing we could see at first was the familiar white tufts from the anti-aircraft, up in the sky, and then she jumped and cried, "there, there my love, I see them, I can see them, there, look, look, there darling," and she tried to point them out to me, through the narrow opening of the shutters, in the direction of the airfield in the east. I could see nothing in the bright blue of the sky, that hurt the eyes and formed fantastic shapes that changed forms, dissolved and reformed in front of my weary straining eyes. Then I saw them, too, small black shapes, dozens of them, heading towards their destination, surrounded by the lacework of the white tufts.

There was something in the sheer strength of their relentless flight, in the drone of their engines, the crackling of the anti-aircraft, that went straight into my head and started doing strange things to me. I felt my body getting excited again, as if in the hands of a mysterious power, as if this very masculine show of strength up there in the sky, as if War itself, were containing me in the one big plan and were pouring out through my own excited masculinity. And then the subterranean shaking from the exploding bombs that fell on the airfield reached us and I went crazy, I felt as if I myself were doing all this, facing alone the whole German army, treading on the enemy, raping him, triumphing in his shame. She must have felt the same, equally excited too – I cannot know how it worked with her – because, suddenly, she turned and looked at me and there was that unmistakable look in her eyes which brought me its own particular message and she said, very simply, "come" and she took me by the hand and led me to the sofa and she lay down and continued to look at me, always the same silent message, and now we both knew that this was it, that the ultimate moment had come that would bind us together for ever and ever, irrevocably, the moment that we would carry in our mind for the rest of our lives, no matter what happened, where we were, the complete union and final stamp on our love that had waited all this time for the moment to be right and the moment was right now, in the midst of War, under the ruthless machines and their sound, the explosions of the bombs, the shaking of the earth – and so I took her and it was easy, she did not hurt, no sound came from her, only she pressed me suddenly with all her strength on top of her as I entered her, kissing my face all over, whispering words I could not understand, I shaking and trembling, not knowing what I was doing nor when I actually finished, everything so immense that even the orgasm could not be felt, feeling her insides, wet and smooth, trapping my body and I knowing that, now, not only was she mine but it was my sole duty in life and my unshakeable decision to do everything that I could to make her as happy as possible and that no one would ever hurt her in the least unless they stepped over my dead body first.

NOBODY PAID ANY ATTENTION TO ME, OF COURSE, LET alone pass over my dead body, nobody even knew of my existence, when the time came... And I did not resist, did not put up any fight – for, what to resist, what to fight against, how can a child fight alone against Evil in its absolute form? I just lived to see it happen, incapable of doing anything but be a part of the nightmare.

They started insidiously and imperceptibly at first, the first steps appearing almost innocent and then becoming more and more obvious, more ruthless as they cared less and less to hide their intentions. I lived and saw it all happen, as the Jews themselves did, incapable in their puzzled minds to grasp the full meaning of what was taking place, believing that every new measure taken against them would be the last, there would be no more, it was humanly impossible for anything more to be done against them, the Jews trying even to laugh at it all, we unable to do the same, stunned and horrified as we were, always wanting to believe that this could not go further, the wickedness and the misery – and yet every day it did go further, if we thought that it was humanly impossible for it to happen, we simply forgot that it was inhumanly possible.

The Star of David was ordered to be shown, in bold design, on the front of every Jewish home or shop or any other premises, and then it was pinned, big and yellow, on their very clothes, thus showing them to the world and, at the same time, cutting them off from it. Their movements were restricted in the town, whole areas and shops and even the trams were forbidden to them. And then that day came when all male Jews were forced to gather in the Liberty Square, and there made to kneel on the ground and stay there still and unmoving, from eight in the morning to two in the afternoon, the young and the old and the ill, even the rabbis, under the relentless sun, the Germans hitting them if they dared move or if they fell from exhaustion, offering no reason for this gathering they had ordered, no explanation, nothing, the only obvious reason being the humiliation and the submission to their whims, an incredible spectacle of an incredible black joke that put the sign of death on one and all, the victims and the perpetrators, and we lived it all, as it was happening, all those hours that it lasted; we saw it with our own eyes and we returned home and the sign of death stamped our own hearts, too, and we now knew that nothing would ever stop them, there would be no end to it but the final end. And I saw it happening, too, and I did not resist and did not put up a fight and a black hatred was cemented inside me that follows me to this day like a shadow.

THE LAST TWO MONTHS WE WERE TOGETHER AS MUCH as it was possible, bound desperately to each other, talking little but communicating more than ever before. We made love almost daily, silently, furiously, trying to give and take as much as we could in the short time that we now knew was left us, knowing now that this was what we would live with in the time to come, the substitute of the life and happiness we had dreamed of together, and for a time had believed in, those two years we had lived together, walking in the air, when what had been given us was more than one could hope to find in a lifetime, and now the time had come to pay the price. *You, my girl with the huge grey eyes, love of all the earth, you, made for love and yet all-pure.* God knows how she did not become pregnant during this time; we never took any precautions, we would not have known how – but even if we had known we still would not have let anything false happen to our love. Nor would she have been saved if she had been with child. With that incredible and proud mentality of their race, her family would still have chosen that they all perish together rather than leave her behind. When the rumours were turned to certainty that the Germans would gather them all and deport them to the concentration camps, Father had suggested to Jack, her Father, to keep Gioconda in hiding when they would have to go – we could hope that we would manage not to be caught. But her parents, though deeply moved by our offer, had absolutely refused to part from her. And when I asked her not to obey them but to stay with us against their will, when I pleaded and begged, when I told her that she had no right to sacrifice her life and our love and our dreams, she replied quietly, and with the peace of death in her voice, that, yes, her life would have no meaning away from me, except for the memories she would carry with her and the love she would continue to feel – but it was impossible for her to abandon her parents and her brothers and her sisters to their fate and stay behind to save herself. In her eyes was all the pain and the despair of the world but her voice was so quiet and determined that I knew I was face to face with Destiny itself and not even my life could change one little bit of it.

THEY TOOK THEM AWAY ONE HOT AFTERNOON. A BIG army lorry came, with three German soldiers and a young officer that talked little. They were methodical and almost polite. The neighbours were looking out of their windows. Children had gathered around the lorry, watching with silent curiosity all that was happening. My parents and I were in their house, to help, to say good-bye. Few words were spoken, a silent frantic activity, tragic in its solemnity and the attention we paid to needless details. They were allowed only a few clothes each, some foodstuff. These were packed in two old suitcases and a clumsily made parcel. Jack and Madame Leonora were doing the packing with the help of Laura and Renée. There was very little that we could do, beyond being there with them. The old grandmother was sitting in her armchair, proud and silent. Aline, more fragile than at any other time and a little scared, was sitting motionless on the edge of the bed. The two boys were outside, together with the other children, curious rather than upset. The officer and the soldiers stood waiting in the garden, patient, looking as if they wanted to apologize. She and I were standing in a corner of the living-room, holding hands, speechless, weak in the knees sick in the stomach dead in our hearts. She had given me her collection of dried flowers, the one that she had made some years ago at school "to keep it for me until I return, to remember me..." I knew the lie of the promise, she knew it, too, only we had to try and believe that she would return or how could we carry on living? I was holding the book lifelessly in one hand, pressing her fingers with the other, her life passing through them on to me, my love and my devotion to her, to carry wherever she would go for ever and ever. I had brought her a golden cross that I used to wear since my early childhood, hung around my neck on a thin chain. I had asked her if she would mind wearing a cross. She had answered that no, she did not mind, perhaps Christ would take care of her, too. I had put it around her neck and she was now holding it in her hand, absently, as we stood there, watching the preparations, the comings and goings of the grown-ups, as they whispered to each other, exchanged advice and instructions, the two men trying to look optimistic and courageous, the two mothers dry, tense and realistic.

At last the moment came when they could not go on pretending that they had things to do still. Everything had been done, finished, all was ready. We stood around, awkward, silent. Then Madame Leonora went round every room, closed the shutters and locked the windows. Very carefully. The house darkened inside. From her dressing-table, in their bedroom, she took an old oblong box of brown leather and she gave it to Mother.

"Would you please keep this for me? I have some jewellery in it that I would hate to fall into strange hands. One of the brooches belongs to my Mother here, one of the rings was my Grandmother's. Will you keep them for me? Or for the girls?... Or... if we decide not to come back when all this is over, if... we like it better there... you know... then keep them for yourself to wear and to remember me. Will you?"

"But of course, yes... my God, yes." Mother's voice was barely audible and her hands were shaking now. Jack stretched, looked all around and pronounced, rather too loudly:

"Well, I think that, after twenty-four years in this little old place, a change will do good to all of us, what? And when we come back, I shall have it all repaired, inside-out, I'll make it as good as new. And I'll plant flowers in the garden and I'll repair the fence and I'll..."

"Jack," his wife interrupted him softly, tenderly, "I think we have to be going. They may start getting impatient," she pointed out at the garden where the Germans were waiting, "and then it won't be pleasant."

"Yes, yes, sure," Jack choked, "I think we must get going," his voice now low. He took a deep breath. "Fine, let's get started then." He looked very tired now. He lifted one of the suitcases, Father took the other, Renée got the bundle. We trotted out, one by one, into the garden.

Madame Leonora locked the front door and handed the key to Mother. Then, they embraced and kissed, not a word not a tear, their faces dry and drawn. They stood holding each other for a long time. Father went up to Jack and put his arms around his shoulders. They touched cheeks, instead of kissing, and stayed so. Father was talking into Jack's ear and he, Jack, kept nodding his head. His eyes were now red and shone with unshed tears. Then Mother and Father kissed the grandmother and, following behind, I kissed her hand. She touched my forehead with her lips and blessed me.

"My poor, poor child," she whispered, "so young and already to be tried so hard, to have to live all this... Don't worry, she will not forget you..." she added unexpectedly and conspiratorially and then I knew that nothing had escaped her all this time, that she knew and, in her infinite wisdom, she approved. A sob choked me but she touched my head lightly and it stopped.

The girls and the two little boys came along and kissed my parents and me. And then Gioconda came and stood in front of me and looked at me for a long time, very intensely. I stepped towards her and she threw herself in my arms and we kissed on the mouth with all our despair and the love and the need, there in front of everyone, no hiding any more, we did not want to hide any more, this our last kiss our declaration of love to the whole world.

And there, with her lips pressed against my ear, she begged me to forgive her for going away, for not having the courage to stay behind, away from her people, she asked me to forgive her for the sorrow she was causing me. She, *she* was begging me to forgive her, *she* was talking about lack of courage. My knees gave.

"My dearest, please stop, for God's sake, I can't stand it, darling please, don't. Whoever else could have had your courage? Look at me, what am I doing? I am standing here, impotent, powerless, miserable, watching you go, watching them take you away and doing nothing but stand here. Me, me, who is going to forgive *me*? Ever?"

She pressed herself upon my body. She whispered into my ear of her love and how great it was, how she would never forget a single one of our moments, how she would think of me all the time.

"Nikos, where are our dreams now, what will become of them?"

"We shall live for our dreams, my love, you see how we must live, we must not be defeated. And you will come back to me, love, my precious love, I shall be living for this from now on. For the day you will come back and there will be no fear around us. Darling, come back." She shook all over, she could not hold back any longer, she started weeping, her sobs coming up from her chest silently, her tears ran and mixed with mine where our faces touched tightly, our last silent communication, the sealing and the confirmation and the farewell – until Madame Leonora came along and put her hand on her shoulder gently and pulled her away and they walked towards the lorry that was waiting.

The soldiers helped them get aboard, then they handed them their luggage and then they got aboard, too, and lifted the rear side of the lorry and fastened the chain. The officer turned to my Father and, unexpectedly and rather incongruously, stood to attention and saluted.

Then he climbed in front, next to the driver, and the lorry started and moved away from us, in the narrow street, came to the corner and turned and went on, on the main road, out of sight now. Its sound continued to reach us for some time and while we could hear it we stayed there and then it faded away and everything was very quiet and we were very much alone. The neighbours had withdrawn from their windows and had closed the shutters. The children had disappeared. We were very much alone as we stood there, in the empty garden of Gioconda's house.

We returned home.

IT WAS ABOUT TEN MONTHS AFTER THE END OF THE War, in the spring of '46, that Rudi made his appearance one evening. He had returned to Greece a few days earlier. He hadn't changed much, physically, except that his skin was darker, not the tan of a healthy man but that hue that comes from overexposure and a hard life – his skin had lost its former shiny smoothness. This, together with a marked change in his manner, gave the impression of an altogether different person. Where, before, he was slim and quick, now he was just underweight with nervous gestures. He talked slowly and deliberately, his manner was guarded, almost sinister. Gone were the laughter, the high spirits, the sparkle. Instead, one could now see a kind of maturity beyond his age, a young man who had lived more than a human lifetime and who had known things that were beyond a man's ability to imagine and understand. His story, as he told it, was short, almost laconic, though heavy with a troubled emotion. He said that the journey to Germany had been a nightmare. He said that Aline had died one month after they had reached the concentration camp and the grandmother four months later. The rest of the family had survived until near the end of the War but were then put to the gas-chambers a few weeks before the arrival of the Russians. He himself was the only one to survive from the whole circle of relatives. They had used him, to the end, in heavy work, they had even forced him to assist with the burning of the bodies of those who had been gassed and were disposed of in the crematoria. A close friend had put Gioconda's body in the furnace. *Her body, oh Lord, her Body. The one that You gave to me to hold in my arms, alive and lively, the body that carried our love inside it, that same love that You gave us. Lord, this body was put in a furnace and was burned into ashes, a furnace made by men to burn people in it. Lord, You are great, indeed, and Your acts are wondrous to behold.*

After this, my memory is very vague as regards the rest of Rudi's story. I only remember that, at one point, I asked him if he knew whether they had done anything else to her while she was alive, whether they had used her for one of their purposes. I remember that he looked at me for a long time before he answered me and then he said that he was certain that nothing of the kind had happened to her. I did not try to guess, then or at any other time, whether he was telling me the truth or was just being kind to me. May God have seen to it, at least, that nothing else happened to her. Mother gave him the jewellery-box that Madame Leonora had given her to keep, for him to do whatever he wanted to do with it. It was obvious that he was in need of money.

We saw him a few more times until he arranged all his affairs and emigrated to the United States, where he had his only living relatives. At first he used to write fairly regularly but gradually, as was only natural, his letters became more and more infrequent and finally they stopped altogether. We have not heard from him for more than fifteen years now. His last letters were optimistic and showed confidence. He had found work with his uncle and he had married a young Jewish girl. He sounded almost happy.

I HAD BEEN DOING MY SERVICE IN THE ARMY FOR ABOUT a year when I took a few days' leave to visit home and see my parents. And then I discovered, accidentally, that her collection of dried flowers, the one she had given me on the day of our separation, was missing from inside the big drawer of my desk where I had kept it all those years. I searched frantically everywhere. It was not to be found. I asked my Mother and she could not remember anything at first but then she did remember that, a few months before, a little cousin of mine had come for a visit and had been fiddling with my things and he had found this collection and had asked permission to take it. My Mother, who did not know anything about its history, and who didn't think I would mind, gave it to him. I went straight to his home to ask for it back. He did not have it any longer. He had exchanged it for some stamps with a school-fellow of his who had then moved, with his parents, to Athens. My cousin did not know his address.

SO NOW THERE IS NOTHING LEFT OF HER. THEIR HOUSE still exists. A sad, forlorn house that is going to ruin. Occupied by a poor, vulgar family, dwarfed by the monstrous blocks of flats that have sprouted all around it, it is the stony expression of a malicious joke of Fate, an evil laughter that had sounded thirty years earlier and had been petrified. The open lot where the grass grew tall and the thyme smelt, is no more. In its space and in the adjacent space of our own home, an ugly building has been built. The big trees, the low walls, the log-cabin – all are gone without a trace behind them.

GIOCONDA IS NOW A DREAM. SOMETIMES I WONDER IF she ever existed and then I ask my parents and my cousins, to make sure. Somewhere in East Germany, a part of her may still survive in the trunk of a tree, in a piece of land. People may have smelt her in a flower, may have drunk her in their wine. The winds, blowing all these years, may have brought her back to Greece and I may have breathed her in, in one last unconscious act of consummated love. The big grey eyes, the soft lips, the smooth skin, the husky voice... The laughter and the sadness and the love that was She.

BIOGRAPHICAL NOTES

NIKOS KOKANTZIS

Nikos Kokantzis was born and raised in Thessaloniki, where he studied medicine. He lived in London for years, and studied psychiatry, specialising in psychoanalysis and psychotherapy. In 1975 he published *Gioconda*, a true story from the time of the Occupation, which won critical acclaim in newspapers and literary journals both in Greece and abroad.

LIST OF TITLES IN
THE "MODERN GREEK WRITERS" SERIES

PETROS ABATZOGLOU *What does Mrs. Freeman want*
  Novel. Translated by Kay Cicellis

ARIS ALEXANDROU *Mission Box*
  Novel. Translated by Robert Crist

NIKOS BAKOLAS *Crossroads*
  Novel. Translated by Caroline Harbouri

SOTIRIS DIMITRIOU *Woof, Woof, Dear Lord*
  Short Stories. Translated by Leo Marshall

MARO DOUKA *Fool's Gold*
  Novel. Translated by Roderick Beaton

EUGENIA FAKINOU *Astradeni*
  Novel. Translated by H. E. Criton

ANDREAS FRANGHIAS *The Courtyard*
  Novel. Translated by Martin McKinsey

COSTIS GIMOSOULIS *Her Night on Red*
  Novel. Translated by Philip Ramp

MARIOS HAKKAS *Heroes' Shrine for Sale or the Elegant Toilet*
Short Stories. Translated by Amy Mims

GIORGOS HEIMONAS *The Builders*
Novel. Translated by Robert Crist

YORGOS IOANNOU *Good Friday Vigil*
Short Stories. Translated by Peter Mackridge and Jackie Willcox

YORGOS IOANNOU *Refugee Capital*
Thessaloniki Chronicles. Translated by Fred A. Reed

IAKOVOS KAMBANELLIS *Mauthausen*
Chronicle. Translated by Gail Holst-Warhaft

NIKOS KOKANTZIS *Gioconda*
Novel. Translated by the author

ALEXANDROS KOTZIAS *Jaguar*
Novel. Translated by H.E. Criton

MENIS KOUMANDAREAS *Koula*
Novel. Translated by Kay Cicellis

MARGARITA LIBERAKI *Three Summers*
Novel. Translated by Karen Van Dyck

GIORGOS MANIOTIS *Two Thrillers*
Translated by Nicholas Kostis

CHRISTOFOROS MILIONIS *Kalamás and Achéron*
Short Stories. Translated by Marjorie Chambers

COSTOULA MITROPOULOU *The Old Curiosity Shop on Tsimiski Street*
Novel. Translated by Elly Petrides

KOSTAS MOURSELAS   *Red Dyed Hair*
  Novel.   Translated by Fred A. Reed

ARISTOTELIS NIKOLAIDIS   *Vanishing-point*
  Novel.   Translated by John Leatham

ALEXIS PANSELINOS   *Betsy Lost*
  Novel.   Translated by Caroline Harbouri

NIKOS-GABRIEL PENTZIKIS   *Mother Salonika*
  Translated by Leo Marshall

SPYROS PLASKOVITIS   *The Façade Lady of Corfu*
  Novel.   Translated by Amy Mims

VANGELIS RAPTOPOULOS   *The Cicadas*
  Novel.   Translated by Fred A. Reed

YANNIS RITSOS   *Iconostasis of Anonymous Saints*
  Novel (?)   Translated by Amy Mims

ARIS SFAKIANAKIS   *The Emptiness Beyond*
  Novel.   Translated by Caroline Harbouri

DIDO SOTIRIOU   *Farewell Anatolia*
  Novel.   Translated by Fred A. Reed

STRATIS TSIRKAS   *Drifting Cities*
  A Trilogy.   Translated by Kay Cicellis

ALKI ZEI   *Achilles' fiancée*
  Novel.   Translated by Gail Holst-Warhaft